Listen...
Can You Hear it?

Written by Shannon Chubbs-Rogers
Illustrated by Megan Strickland

Shannon Rogers

Produced by:

FriesenPress
Suite 300 – 852 Fort Street
Victoria, BC, Canada V8W 1H8

www.friesenpress.com

Distributed to the trade by The Ingram Book Company

To my two beautiful kids,
Daylin & Isabella.
You make me so happy, and proud to be
your mommy.
Remember, you can do anything
and you are loved, so very much.

To my husband, Kerry.
Thank you for always supporting me.
You are a great dad and I love you
more than I can ever say.

To Rory, Millie, Logan, Brett, Whitney, Avery,
Loren, Alanna, Daniel, Ryder, Rayn and to
all of you beautiful goofballs that make me
smile every day.

Thank you to all my friends and family
for supporting me and always cheering me on.

This book is also dedicated to all the
people that live on, or are from
The Lower North Shore!

Listen...can you hear it? It's the beautiful sound of the Shore. It's a magical place so get ready; it's like nothing you've seen before.

All tucked away in the north, most people don't know that it's there. It's my home on the Coast and it's special; so special that I feel I should share.

The quiet small towns and salty blue sea, the roads... they don't go very far.

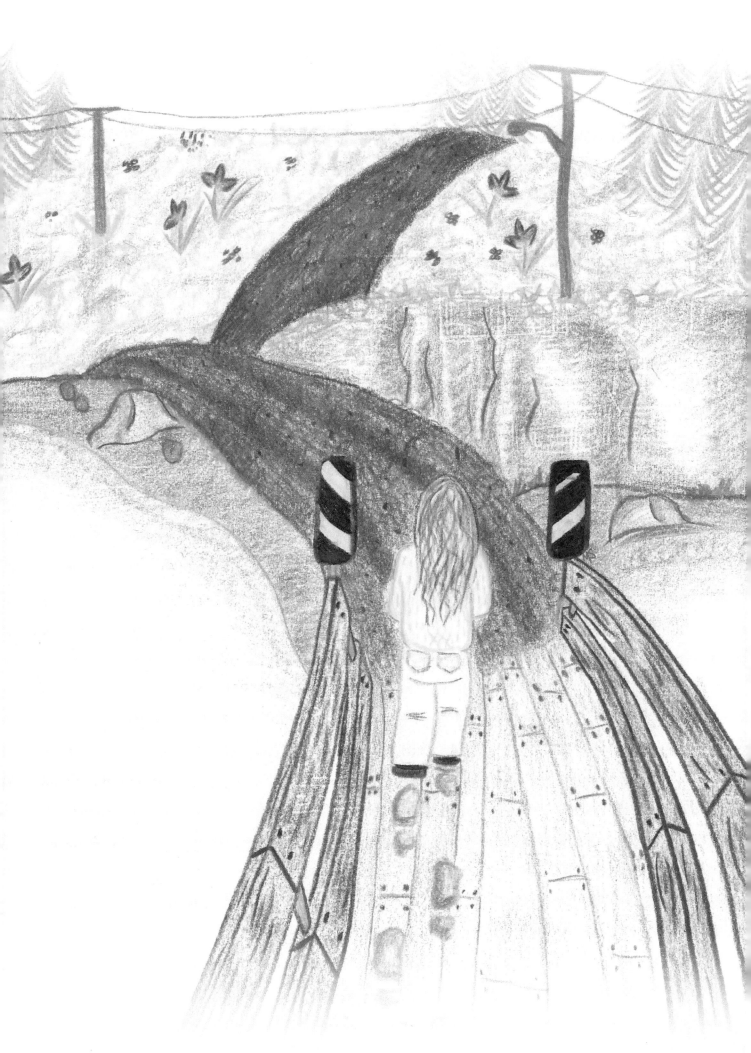

You can come here by Ski-
doo, by plane or by boat,
but you cannot come here
by a car.

In the summer we like to go fishing, lots of ways you can fish in the sea.

You can use rods, nets and traps or go for a "jig," on the water is where I feel free.

Sea gulls they fly over head, their cries are a familiar sound. Salt on my skin, the sun and the wind, the whales they swim all around.

We walk all over the islands, to find where the wild baby birds sleep. We collect sea glass, pretty rocks and white shells; these are memories that I'll always keep.

Have you ever gone picking wild berries? I bet you haven't picked berries like this. There are blueberries, raspberries, red berries and currants, but bakeapples are number one on my list!

When the leaves start to change and there's a chill in the air, it always makes me feel glad. What I love to do best, above all of the rest, is to go hunting with my grandpa and dad.

Winter time brings all kinds of adventures. Ski-doing is my other number one. The roads are all closed, and everyone knows, that winter on the Coast is really fun.

The ponds, they all freeze over, and the daytime it gets very short. When the day is all done, you can still have some fun, and build the biggest snow fort.

We go camping and ice-fishing in winter.

To stay warm the grown-ups cut wood.

We all play ice hockey, our parents cheer and drink coffee, and we all have fun like kids should.

Here we don't have hustle and bustle. It's quiet, our home by the sea. Feel free to drop by, I'll be sure to say Hi. There's no place that I'd rather be.

La Tabatirère,
Québec, Canada

Mutton Bay, Québec, Canada

Groupe
Desgagnés inc.

Bella Desgagnés

CPSIA information can be obtained
at www.ICGtesting.com
Printed in the USA
LVIC070438180513
334368LV00003BA